This book should be returned to any branch of the
Lancashire County Library on or before the date shown

13 SEP 2019

- 2 MAY 2018

1 4 MAY 2018

2 5 JUL 2018

4 SEP 2018

D0808345

- 3 JUN 2

2 3 AUG 2019

Lancashire County Library,
County Hall Complex,
1st floor Christ Church Precinct,
Preston, PR1 8XJ

www.lancashire.gov.uk/libraries

LL1(A)

Look out for:

Zoe's Rescue ZOO

The Giggly Giraffe

Amelia Cobb

Illustrated by
Sophy Williams

nosy
crow

With special thanks to Natalie Doherty

First published in the UK in 2018 by Nosy Crow Ltd
The Crow's Nest, 14 Baden Place
Crosby Row, London SE1 1YW

Nosy Crow and associated logos are trademarks and/or
registered trademarks of Nosy Crow Ltd

Text copyright © Hothouse Fiction, 2018
Illustrations © Sophy Williams, 2018

A CIP catalogue record for this book will be available from the British Library

Printed and bound in the UK by Clays Ltd, St Ives Plc

Papers used by Nosy Crow are made from wood grown in sustainable forests.

ISBN: 978 0 85763 985 1

www.nosycrow.com

Chapter One
A New Baby

Zoe Parker ran down the red-brick path of the Rescue Zoo with a huge grin on her face. "Mum!" she shouted, waving her arms. "Mum, guess what?"

Lucy Parker popped her head round the door of the zoo hospital, where she was working that morning. "I'm here, Zoe! What's happened?" she asked.

"It's Jewel!" Zoe cried.
"Her baby is on
the way!"

"That's great
news," Lucy
smiled. "Wait
there, Zoe – I'll
be out in just
a minute."

Zoe bounced
up and down
on the path
outside the
zoo hospital
as her mum
quickly packed
all the things she would need in case
she had to help deliver the new baby –
a giraffe!

Zoe wasn't just a visitor to the zoo. She actually lived there! Her Great-Uncle Horace had started the zoo a long time ago as a home for any animals that were lost, poorly or in danger. Zoe's mum was the zoo vet, and she and Zoe lived in a cosy little cottage at the edge of the zoo.

Zoe loved her amazing home, and her all-time favourite thing about living in a zoo was when a new animal arrived.

Jewel the giraffe was expecting her first baby, and Zoe had been looking forward to the little calf arriving for such a long time. The other zoo animals were really excited too!

"I'm ready, let's go," said Lucy, stepping outside and swinging a big bag full of special equipment and medicine on to her shoulder.

Together they raced down the path,
past the wolves and the polar bears.
As they passed the pot-bellied pigs, one
of them pushed his snout through a gap
in the fence and gave a grunt. "Yes, the
baby giraffe is coming!" whispered Zoe,
dropping back a little so that her mum
wouldn't hear her. "I'll let you know as

soon as there's any news, Polly!"

Living in the Rescue Zoo wasn't the only special thing about Zoe. She had a very unusual gift – she could talk to animals! It made growing up in a zoo even more fun – although Zoe couldn't let anyone else know her secret. Not even her mum or Great-Uncle Horace knew!

Zoe caught up with her mum again, and when they reached the giraffe enclosure, a tiny furry creature was perched on the gate waiting for them. As soon as he saw Zoe, his fluffy ears pricked up excitedly.

"Hello, Meep," Zoe said as he jumped from the gate on to her shoulder.

Meep was a grey mouse lemur with big golden eyes and a long, curling tail. Of all the animals in the zoo, he was Zoe's most special friend. "I've been keeping an eye on things, Zoe," he chattered importantly. "The baby giraffe hasn't been born yet. But Theo, the giraffe keeper, is here. And someone else has just arrived too," he added happily.

"Someone else? Who do you mean?" asked Zoe, puzzled. "Another zoo keeper?"

Meep shook his head. "Go and look, Zoe," he squeaked.

Zoe followed her mum through the gate and into the giraffe enclosure. She always thought it was one of the nicest parts of the zoo, designed to look just like the African savannah, where giraffes in the wild would live. There were juicy acacia trees dotted around, a gurgling stream winding its way through the middle of the enclosure, and a large watering hole where the giraffes could have a drink and cool down in the summer.

Theo, the Rescue Zoo giraffe keeper, was standing on the other side of the enclosure from Jewel, whose belly was looking very big and round because of the baby inside it. Next to Theo was a man with wild white hair and twinkling brown eyes, wearing dusty safari clothes. On his shoulder perched a beautiful deep-blue bird with a curved black and yellow beak.

"Great-Uncle Horace!" gasped Zoe, rushing over to hug him. "I thought you were in Africa."

Great-Uncle Horace was a famous explorer and animal expert, and he spent most of his time travelling around the world meeting different animals. The bird on his shoulder was Kiki, his hyacinth macaw, who went everywhere with him.

"I was!" laughed Great-Uncle Horace. "In fact, I was visiting a herd of wild giraffes in a very hot place called Tanzania. But I knew that our own baby giraffe would be arriving soon, so I decided to fly back to the zoo and surprise you all. It seems like I've got here just in time!"

Jewel began pacing about in circles on her slender legs.

"This is what happens when the baby is almost here!" whispered Zoe to Meep, who nodded. Zoe had been reading all about baby giraffes!

She and Meep stood back with Great-Uncle Horace, Lucy and Theo as they watched Jewel's baby being born. First Zoe could see four hooves, then four spindly legs. Finally the calf dropped to the ground, shook its head and looked around.

"Oh, wow, what a gorgeous baby," Zoe sighed, hugging Meep happily. She watched as her mum went over to the calf and gently checked it. "It's a boy!" Lucy called to everyone.

"Yay! A boy like me," chirped Meep, looking very pleased.

Zoe giggled. "Can we come over and have a look?" she called to her mum.

"Of course! He's beautiful," Lucy replied with a smile.

Feeling very excited, Zoe approached the new baby, who gazed at her curiously with his big black eyes. Even though he was much smaller than his mum, the giraffe's skinny legs with their knobbly knees were already much longer than Zoe's.

The little giraffe had large, fluffy ears, and two funny, furry stumps on the top of his head, called ossicones. His body was covered with a patchwork of golden-brown splodges of different sizes and shapes. Zoe knew that every giraffe's coat patterns were different, a bit like the way every human had their own unique set of fingerprints.

"What shall we call him?" asked Theo.

"Zoe, you're usually very good at picking names," said Great-Uncle Horace.

"Why don't you think of something?"

Zoe did her best not to giggle. Her mum and Great-Uncle Horace thought she was good at picking names for new animals, but it wasn't really true. She usually asked the animal their name, and then pretended she'd come up with it herself! She couldn't tell her mum and Great-Uncle Horace that, of course. This time she really *would* get to pick the new giraffe's name, because this baby was too young to have a name yet.

"How about . . . Jamie?" she suggested.

The baby giraffe's eyes lit up, and Zoe could tell he liked it.

"Perfect!" said Lucy. "Jamie it is. Look — he's already trying to walk!"

The little calf put his hooves flat on the ground and pushed himself up.

Now that he was standing, Zoe could see
how tall he was already – even taller than
Great-Uncle Horace! His legs wobbled
back and forth
underneath
him, and
Zoe was sure
he would fall
straight over.

"He's
determined!"
chuckled
Great-Uncle
Horace.
"And
baby
giraffes
need
to be.

After all, if this baby had been born in the wild, it would be very important for him to learn to walk straight away — because of all the wild animals that might attack him, like lions, hyenas and leopards. That's why baby giraffes start walking within just an hour of them being born — so they can escape from any predators. It's to help them survive. It's very clever."

"Luckily, there's no danger of this baby meeting any of *our* lions, hyenas or leopards," whispered Zoe to Meep, thinking of the enclosures on the other side of the Rescue Zoo where those animals lived.

As Jamie lifted one hoof to take a shaky step, everyone cheered and clapped.

"Well done, Jamie! That's brilliant!" cried Zoe.

The baby giraffe managed another few wobbly steps, but he was so unsteady that his legs seemed to take him backwards instead of forwards. Everyone laughed as he stumbled around — which made Jamie laugh too. Zoe grinned as the little calf giggled and squealed, wobbling around on his brand-new legs.

"He's so funny!" chattered Meep, jumping down from Zoe's shoulder and copying the baby. "It's like his legs are made of jelly!"

As Meep pretended to wobble around, the giraffe giggled even harder. Zoe could already tell that the zoo's newest arrival had a good sense of humour.

"Excuse me, what is going on here?" barked a cross voice from behind Zoe. "I'm trying to do some important work in my office, but all I can hear is noise."

Zoe whirled around to see the zoo's manager, Mr Pinch, marching into the enclosure. He looked really grumpy ... but then Mr Pinch *always* looked really grumpy!

"Ah, Mr Pinch, I'm so sorry you were disturbed," said Great-Uncle Horace. "But it's for a very good reason. You see, we are just celebrating the safe arrival of the Rescue Zoo's newest resident."

Mr Pinch wrinkled up his nose as he watched the baby giraffe stumble around. "He's not very good at walking, is he?" he said disapprovingly.

"He's only just been born!" Zoe exclaimed indignantly. Mr Pinch was always complaining about the animals, usually about how messy they were!

"Well, anyway, now that I've found you all, I have some very exciting news to share," announced Mr Pinch, completely ignoring Zoe and the giraffe. "I have decided to enter the Rescue Zoo into a very important competition – the

Best Zoo Competition. If we win we'll be given the Best Zoo Award. It's a wonderful award – all shiny and gold. It would look perfect in my office."

"The Best Zoo Award. That sounds very interesting, Mr Pinch!" replied Great-Uncle Horace. "Please tell us more."

"A team of judges will visit the zoo for an inspection," Mr Pinch told him. "They'll look at our enclosures and our animals, and decide whether they think we deserve the prize. We'll be competing against the two other zoos in the region." He put his hands on his hips and looked very determined. "But I'm going to make sure that the Rescue Zoo wins. I don't care what it takes. I want that prize!"

Zoe looked at Meep and smiled. It

wasn't often that she agreed with Mr Pinch, but this time she did. It would be great if the Rescue Zoo won the Best Zoo Award!

Chapter Two
The Very Silly Giraffe

Early the next morning, Zoe's eyes flew open as a loud trumpeting noise burst through her bedroom window.

"What's going on?" she asked sleepily, sitting up and glancing at the clock on her bedroom wall. "It's only six o'clock – and today's Sunday. Normally the elephants don't wake us up for at least another hour."

At the foot of her bed, Meep was rubbing his eyes and yawning. "I was having a lovely dream about eating a big, delicious banana," he said, patting his tummy. "It was such a good dream, Zoe. I wish I hadn't woken up!"

Zoe giggled and scooped her little friend up for a cuddle. Meep was always hungry, and loved bananas most of all. "Never mind," she said. "Now that we're awake we can go and have breakfast – and you really can have a banana, just like in your dream. Then let's go and find out why the elephants are making such a racket."

After quickly getting dressed, Zoe and Meep ran downstairs. As Zoe and Meep ate their breakfast, they could hear the noisy trumpeting sound from outside again. Meep's little ears pricked up every time the sound floated through the window. Zoe giggled as he looked in confusion at his banana, then at the front door of the cottage, then back to his banana again. "Meep, what are you doing?" she asked, leaning over to stroke Meep's soft fur.

"I'm trying to decide what I want most," explained Meep. "To finish my banana, or to find out what's going on outside."

"Well, you've only got three bites left," Zoe told him, laughing. "Finish up quickly and then let's go."

Meep stuffed the last three bits of banana in his mouth, making his cheeks puff up like a hamster's, while

Zoe washed up her cereal bowl. Then Meep jumped on Zoe's shoulder and they headed outside. They followed the trumpeting sound all the way to the elephant enclosure, and peered inside to see what was going on.

All the elephants were crowded at one side of their enclosure, waving their trunks in the air. They were looking through the fence into the enclosure next to theirs – which belonged to the giraffes. On the other side of the fence, Jamie the baby giraffe was waving his long slender neck from side to side, and giggling. The elephants trumpeted noisily again, and Zoe called out to one of them – a friendly, gentle male with huge tusks.

"Edgar, what's going on?" she asked, waving him over.

Edgar plodded over to the fence and said hello to Zoe by patting her head with the tip of his trunk. Then he gave a low rumble and used his trunk to point at Jamie. Zoe started chuckling.

"Now I understand, Meep! The elephants are *laughing* – at Jamie!" she said. "The funny giraffe is pretending to be an elephant, like them. Look at how he's waving his neck, as if it's a trunk!"

Meep started giggling himself as he watched Jamie having fun. "Maybe I can pretend to be an elephant too, Zoe. Watch," he chattered, and he lifted his long curly tail high into the air and swung it from side to side. "This is *my* trunk!"

Edgar let out a low rumble of laughter as the cheeky lemur pretended to be an elephant. Zoe burst out giggling too. But then a sharp voice interrupted her.

"Honestly, I think everyone apart from me in this entire zoo has gone mad!" snapped Mr Pinch as he marched over to them. He frowned at Zoe and Meep. "Why are you encouraging the animals to be so loud and naughty? I won't have it!"

"They're playing," explained Zoe, trying

her best not to lose her temper with him.

"Playing!" Mr Pinch tutted crossly.
"The animals can't play at a time like
this! We've got the Best Zoo Award to
think of. The judges are going to arrive at
the Rescue Zoo next Saturday for their
inspection and everything must be perfect.
The paths and flowerbeds must be neat,
the enclosures must be spick and span,
and the animals *must* all be on their very
best behaviour!" He glared through the
fence at the trumpeting elephants. "This
sort of silliness just won't do."

Zoe rolled her eyes, but Mr Pinch didn't
seem to notice. "Now, as you're here, Zoe,
I've got a job for you," the grumpy zoo
manager continued.

Oh no! thought Zoe. Usually Mr Pinch
gave out very boring jobs. Zoe didn't

mind working hard, because it was good practice for being a zoo keeper herself when she was grown up. But Mr Pinch's jobs for Zoe were usually the ones that *didn't* involve the animals, because he

thought those should only be done by real, grown-up keepers and not little girls. He normally told her to pick up litter, weed the plants or clean the windows.

So she couldn't help breathing a sigh of relief as Mr Pinch pointed to Jamie and said, "I need to take that giraffe over to the zoo hospital. Your mum wants to give him a check-up. Could you lead him for me, please? I don't want him slobbering all over my nice clean uniform."

This was a job that Zoe didn't mind doing at all! "OK, Mr Pinch," she said.

As Mr Pinch waited on the path, Zoe reached for the necklace she was wearing. At the end of the chain was a small silver charm in the shape of a paw print. Zoe held it against a small panel in the gate of the giraffe enclosure and, with a click, the gate swung open.

"My magic necklace!" Zoe said, winking at Meep. The special charm opened every gate, fence and door in the whole zoo! Great-Uncle Horace had given it to Zoe for her birthday, when he had decided she was old enough to find her way around the zoo by herself. It was the most precious thing Zoe owned, and she wore it every day.

The little giraffe looked curiously at Zoe as she and Meep stepped inside the enclosure.

"Hi, Jamie," said Zoe, smiling. "We haven't met properly yet, because there were so many people around when you arrived yesterday. My name's Zoe, and this is Meep. We live here at the zoo, just like you!"

Jamie was very excited to learn that Zoe could understand animals, and came over to her to say hello properly. He lowered his long neck so that he could nuzzle Zoe's face with his soft, silky nose, and then did the same to Meep.

"It's time for you to have a check-up at the zoo hospital," Zoe explained to him. "My mum just wants to make sure you're happy and healthy. She's the zoo vet, so she looks after all the animals here.

The hospital's just down the path — not
very far. And you'll be able to see a bit
more of the zoo on the way."

Jamie bleated excitedly, and Zoe led the
baby giraffe out of his enclosure, making
sure she closed the gate properly behind
them.

"Come along!" Mr Pinch called bossily
as he marched off ahead of them.

But as Zoe started following him, she
heard the elephants trumpeting noisily
again.

The paths were starting to fill up with
zoo visitors now, who were all chatting
curiously about the funny noises the
elephants were making.

"It sounds a bit like a brass band!" said
one lady.

"And now it sounds like a storm's

coming," laughed a man, as a howl and a roar rang out.

Zoe realised that the noises were spreading to the other animals! She heard another high-pitched howl from close by, and realised that it was Shadow the wolf pup. Then there was a huge roar from Leonard and Rory, the Rescue Zoo lions, as Zoe, Meep and Jamie passed their savannah enclosure.

The chimpanzees began screeching as they walked past their home, and as they got closer to the bats, Zoe saw the whole colony swooping around in circles, chittering and squeaking as loudly as they could.

And it wasn't just the animals making all the noise any more. The zoo visitors were chuckling too, and Zoe saw lots

of people holding up their phones and
cameras to take pictures. Thankfully
Mr Pinch had marched so far ahead he
hadn't realised what was happening.

"What's going on?" Zoe asked. "Why
is everyone laughing?"

"That's why!" chirped Meep, pointing
at Jamie.

Behind them, the little giraffe was
stumbling down the path, his knees
wobbling and knocking together with
every step he took. He lurched from
one side of the path to the other, almost
crashing into the fence once or twice. But
he didn't seem to mind. In fact, he was
giggling along with all the other animals!

"His walking's even worse than yesterday, Zoe!" laughed Meep, shaking his head.

Zoe smiled at the little giraffe's antics, but secretly she felt a bit worried. Meep was right – Jamie *did* seem to have got even more clumsy than he'd been the day before. Something didn't feel right. Surely his walking should be getting better every day – not worse?

Chapter Three
Planning the Parade

At school the next day, Zoe told all her friends about the zoo's adorable new arrival.

"You actually watched him being born?" gasped her friend Jack. "That's amazing, Zoe! I wish I could see something like that."

Zoe's teacher, Miss Hawkins, was very

interested in hearing about Jamie too.
After lunch, she surprised the class by
showing them all a film on the Internet
of a baby giraffe in the wild taking its first
shaky steps. "Everyone gather round and
watch," she said, clicking 'play' on the film.

All Zoe's classmates crowded around the
computer and watched as the baby giraffe
moved its long, skinny legs forward, one
at a time. At first it stumbled and wobbled,
and the class gasped as it almost tumbled
over – but quickly the little animal seemed
to get the hang of it, and was walking
slowly and steadily along in no time.

"See how quickly giraffes learn to
walk?" Miss Hawkins asked the class, and
everyone nodded. "Zoe, I'm sure you can
tell us why."

"It's so that they can run away from

predators, like lions and hyenas," explained Zoe, remembering what Great-Uncle Horace had told her when Jamie was born.

"That's right. They're very smart creatures indeed," said Miss Hawkins, smiling at Zoe.

"I can't believe you have a cute baby giraffe living right next to your house, Zoe," sighed Zoe's friend Nicola wistfully. "You're so, so lucky."

Zoe thought so too! But seeing how quickly the baby giraffe in the film had got the hang of walking made her think of Jamie's strange behaviour yesterday. Suddenly she felt worried. Jamie's walking was supposed to be getting better and better, but it wasn't. What if there was something wrong with his legs?

For the rest of the day, she found it hard to concentrate on her schoolwork, wondering if Jamie was doing any better today.

When she got back to the zoo that afternoon, Meep was perched on the gates at the zoo entrance. "Zoe, I've been waiting for you," her little friend chirped excitedly. "Quick, come and see what Jamie's doing." He bounced down nimbly on to the path and started scampering in the direction of the giraffe enclosure, with Zoe following him.

When they arrived at the enclosure, Zoe heard a funny, high-pitched squawking sound. *What* is *that?* she thought. *It's not the elephants today – and it's not Jamie either.*

She used her special necklace to open the gate, and she and Meep slipped inside.

Across the enclosure, Zoe could see Jamie standing next to the watering hole. He was bending his long neck down to the water so that he could have a drink.

"Oh, that's good, Meep!" said Zoe, pleased. "Jamie's learned what the watering hole is for."

"Hmm," Meep smiled mysteriously.

As Zoe watched, Jamie stretched his neck further and further over the water, and his legs started to wobble. "Oh no! I think Jamie's leaning too far over. He's about to lose his balance!" said Zoe. She started running forward, and saw Jewel trotting over to the waterhole too, bleating anxiously at her calf to be careful.

With a huge splash, the baby giraffe toppled into the water!

Zoe gasped. "Quick, Meep – we'd better go and ask for help from some of the zoo keepers!"

But to Zoe's surprise, Meep burst out laughing – and the same strange, high-pitched squawking from before broke out around the enclosure. She looked up and saw a flock of birds perched in the acacia trees, watching Jamie, all shaking their feathers as they laughed and squawked together.

Jamie climbed out of the waterhole, giggling and shaking droplets from his neck, coat and tail.

"He's OK!" Zoe exclaimed, feeling really relieved. "He did it on purpose!"

"He's been doing it all afternoon," Meep explained. "All the other animals think it's brilliant. He's so funny, Zoe.

I love Jamie!"

Zoe smiled at her friend. She loved the playful little calf too, but she was also worried about him. What if he'd really hurt himself? Parts of the waterhole were quite deep, and there were some big rocks that Jamie could have cut or scratched himself on. Plus, all the other animals in the zoo were getting overexcited – and Zoe knew that Mr Pinch was going to get very cross if that carried on!

She watched as Jewel lowered her long neck and spoke quietly to her baby. Then the older giraffe nudged Jamie back to the edge of the watering hole and took a drink herself, balancing carefully on her slender legs as she did so. As Jamie leaned forward and had a drink too, Jewel watched closely.

"Look, Meep! Jewel's teaching Jamie how to do it without falling in," Zoe said, feeling very pleased.

But a second later, a giggling Jamie splashed into the waterhole again! Jewel huffed crossly, while Meep held his tummy and spluttered with laughter.

Zoe bit her lip anxiously. "Meep, I'm glad Jamie's having so much fun at the zoo – and he's making you and all the other animals laugh," she said. "But maybe we need to show him how to be a little bit more sensible and *still* have fun?"

But Meep didn't answer. He was too busy giggling.

After dinner that evening, Zoe was helping her mum clear the table when there was a knock on the door. Lucy went to answer it. "Oh, it's you, Mr Pinch!" she said with a smile. "Come in."

Mr Pinch stepped inside the cottage.

He spotted Meep perching on the dinner table and frowned. "No wonder that little troublemaker never learns any manners, if he's allowed to sit on the table," he commented. Meep stuck his tongue out at Mr Pinch, and somehow Zoe managed to hide her smile.

"Oh, Meep can be cheeky at times but he's as good as gold really," Lucy told him. "Anyway, what can we do for you, Mr Pinch?"

"I'm here to talk to you about the
Best Zoo competition," Mr Pinch said
in his bossiest voice. "I've been secretly
visiting the other zoos that have entered
the competition, to see what we're up
against."

"What do you mean, *secretly* visiting
them?" Zoe asked.

"Well, I couldn't let them know it was
me, so I had to go in disguise," Mr Pinch
replied.

"You went in disguise?" A picture of
Mr Pinch in a pair of dark glasses and a
fake moustache and beard popped into
Zoe's head. She had to bite her lip to
stop herself from laughing. "I think that's
called *spying*," she whispered to Meep,
who sniggered behind his paws.

51

"First I went to Tall Tails Zoo. They won the Best Zoo Award last year," said Mr Pinch. "They have a huge paddock full of wild ponies that have been rescued. Visitors can go right up to the ponies and feed them by hand. Apparently people love it, although I can't think why. I can't stand the thought of a pony slobbering all over me – yuck!" He shuddered. "Then I took a trip to Chestnut Creek Zoo. They've won the award three times, which, if you ask me, is just greedy! They have a huge glass dome with a miniature rainforest inside it, full of tropical wildlife. It was much too hot for my liking, but it seemed very popular, I suppose." He pulled a face.

"They both sound wonderful," said Lucy, smiling. "Don't they, Zoe? Well, I suppose we'll just have to try our best on Saturday—"

"Anyway, I've come up with a brilliant way of making sure we beat them both," interrupted Mr Pinch. "Something that doesn't involve slobbering ponies or tropical heat. When the judges arrive, we're going to hold an animal parade. With the help of our keepers, the animals will march through the zoo, one by one. It will be perfect! And no other zoo will be doing it," he added smugly.

"That's a very interesting idea, Mr Pinch," Lucy replied thoughtfully. "What about our more dangerous animals though? How will they take part?"

"Oh, well, of course we won't be able to include every animal in the parade," said Mr Pinch. "The lions and the crocodiles, for example, will stay in their enclosures, but we'll still include them in some way. Perhaps we'll give them some new, special toys that will help the judges to see how fascinating they are. But only the safest and most well-behaved animals will walk in the parade, like the monkeys, the elephants, the parrots and the giraffes."

Meep let out a squeal of laughter and Mr Pinch gave him a stern look. He just thought Meep was making lots of noise!

The giraffes! thought Zoe. As much as she loved Jamie the giraffe, he certainly wasn't one of the zoo's most well-behaved animals. And if he took part in a parade, where lots of other animals and people would be watching him, Zoe just knew he'd do his best to make everyone laugh. And then all the other animals would get overexcited and everything would get very noisy and messy. *This could go very, very badly*, she thought to herself. *Very badly indeed!*

Chapter Four
Food Fight!

A couple of days later, Zoe and Meep were helping the zoo keepers to sweep, scrub and polish every corner of the zoo. The judges of the Best Zoo Award were visiting in just a few days and Mr Pinch had decided that all the enclosures should be cleaned and tidied. "To win the Best Zoo Award the zoo must look its best!"

he had announced.

As soon as she'd got home from school, Zoe had watered the flowers that lined the zoo path. Then she'd helped to put a fresh coat of paint on three fences. Now she was cleaning up a big muddy puddle outside the hippo enclosure.

As she swirled her mop in her bucket of soapy water, she smiled at the smallest hippo in the family, Henry, who was watching her with bright, eager eyes from the other side of the fence.

It was Henry who had made the puddle Zoe was cleaning up — he loved splashing in the muddy watering hole in his enclosure, and it always made a big mess.

"Try not to splash mud over the fence now, Henry," Zoe whispered once she'd finished. "At least until after the judges have visited on Saturday!"

Next, Zoe and Meep went to the monkey enclosure, where Annie, the monkey keeper, was tidying up. "Can we help?" called Zoe through the fence.

"That would be wonderful, Zoe," replied Annie. "Why don't you grab that broom and sweep up the empty peanut shells from the ground?"

Zoe brushed the shells into a tidy pile. Then

she and Annie started to pick up the old banana skins and put them in a bin bag.

"We're almost there, I think," said Annie, smiling at Zoe. "Thanks for helping out, Zoe. I don't think this enclosure has ever looked so spotless!"

As Zoe picked up the last banana skin, there was a noisy hooting sound from above her head, where the Rescue Zoo monkeys were perched in the treetops. Zoe glanced up to see what they were laughing at.

"It's Jamie!" chattered Meep, pointing to the giraffe enclosure across the path. "Look, he's trying to climb a tree – just like the monkeys!"

Zoe peered over the fence to get a better look at the funny little giraffe. He was galloping around an acacia tree,

jumping as high as he could against the trunk and then tumbling to the ground. Every time he fell, the baby giraffe burst out laughing – and so did the monkeys!

Zoe smiled, but she couldn't help feeling anxious. Jamie was still only a few days old. What if he bruised or cut himself, or twisted one of his ankles?

She was relieved to see Jewel walking over to Jamie and speaking quietly into his ear. *She's trying to get him to stop*, she thought. *His mum doesn't want him to hurt himself either.*

"Jewel seems so calm compared to her baby, doesn't she, Zoe?" said Annie, nodding at Jewel and Jamie.

Zoe nodded, watching the graceful way Jewel moved around. "Jamie has so much energy," she said.

"Baby giraffes always do," Annie said with a smile. "Did you know they only need two or three hours' sleep a day? A human baby needs sixteen or seventeen hours."

"Wow!" said Zoe.

"Only two or three hours sleep a day!" Meep chattered in Zoe's ear, looking amazed. "I can't imagine that. Apart from eating, sleeping is my favourite thing to do!"

Zoe watched as Jewel nudged Jamie towards the branches of the tree and showed him how to pull some leaves off to eat. Jamie ate a few mouthfuls and his mum nodded happily. Then he glanced mischievously at the monkeys.

"Uh-oh," said Zoe. "I think Jamie's about to cause trouble again!"

The little giraffe pulled another mouthful of leaves off the tree – but this time, instead of eating them, he swung his long neck towards the monkeys and let go of the leaves. They scattered all over the path, and some flew over the fence and into the monkeys' enclosure – just where Zoe had finished sweeping up!

"Naughty Jamie!" said Zoe, as the little giraffe burst into giggles.

"Look, Zoe! The monkeys!" cried Meep.

Zoe looked up at the treetops, where the monkeys were still perched. They were whispering and chattering excitedly to one another. Then one of them – a cheeky-looking capuchin monkey – grabbed a banana from a wooden platform, where Annie usually left food for them. He flung the banana as hard

as he could, over the path – and into the
giraffe enclosure, where it splattered on
the ground!

"Food fight!" squealed Meep, bouncing
up and down.

Zoe gasped as all the monkeys grabbed
whatever food they could find and began
throwing it around, squawking and

hooting happily. She managed to duck
just in time as a banana went whizzing
past her head. In no time at all there
were soggy bits of fruit and messy
peanuts all over the enclosure and the
path outside.

"Oh no," sighed Annie, staring at the
mess. "And after all our hard work, Zoe.

We'll have to start all over again! Those naughty, messy monkeys."

Zoe shook her head. "It was Jamie who started it," she said, looking over at the baby giraffe, who was almost falling over with laughter. She bit her lip. Jamie *was* very funny, and she was glad he was happy and settling into life at the zoo so well. But sometimes he was just a bit *too* cheeky!

The next day Zoe arrived home from school just as Mr Pinch decided to call a parade practice.

"The judges will be here in two days' time," Mr Pinch announced sternly into a loudspeaker. "We need to make sure all the animals are ready. I don't want any of them misbehaving on the day."

Mr Pinch ordered the zoo keepers to bring all the animals out of their enclosures, and line them up in order of size. "Smallest animals first!" he called bossily. "We should start with the pygmy shrews, and then the littlest marmosets, and then on to the monkeys."

"What about the insects, Mr Pinch?" asked one of the keepers politely. "We have lots of very tiny ants and spiders at the zoo."

Mr Pinch wrinkled his nose and shook his head. "Ughh! No, I don't want any creepy-crawlies in my parade," he said. "What if the judges don't like them? No, it's cute animals only!"

Zoe frowned and saw the zoo keepers do the same. Lots of people treated insects and spiders very unfairly because they

looked a bit scary sometimes. She thought
it was really unkind of Mr Pinch not
to let them take part in the parade. But
she could tell from his stern face that he
wasn't going to be argued with today!

One by one, the animals were put into
a long line. Zoe couldn't help smiling as
she watched the different animals chatter
happily to one another. They were excited
to be making new friends with animals
they never usually saw around the zoo.
Maybe this parade is a good idea after all, she
thought.

"Now, let's go!" Mr Pinch barked into
his loudspeaker. "I want the animals to
make one full circuit around the zoo in
a neat, tidy and well-behaved way," he
added firmly. "Every animal must stay in
line and there's to be no running, trotting

or galloping. And definitely no monkey business." He shot the monkeys a warning stare.

With the help of the keepers – and Zoe, who whispered encouragingly to all the animals as they passed her – the parade began slowly making its way along the path. Zoe was very impressed with how well behaved the smaller animals were. "That's brilliant! You're all doing so well," she told the ring-tailed lemurs as they trooped past in a neat line. "Keep up the good work!" she added as the pandas padded by. Even the mischievous panda cubs, Chi Chi and Mei Mei, were trotting along together, squeaking excitedly about the parade. "You two are behaving beautifully!" whispered Zoe, smiling at them. "Well done!"

As the parade continued, the animals
got bigger and bigger – and Zoe began
to hear a commotion coming from
the end of the line. She glanced at
Meep, whose clever ears had pricked
up, listening carefully. "It sounds like
laughing," he chirped, puzzled. "But I
can't tell which animal it is. It sounds like
. . . lots of *different* animals laughing at the
same time!"

"Let's go and take a look," Zoe said.
They walked towards the very end of

the parade line. Zoe saw that the zoo
keepers who were supervising this part
of the parade looked quite stressed and
anxious. "What's happening?" she asked
one of them.

"The animals won't walk in a straight
line," the keeper explained. "And we can't
work out why. Suddenly they all started
wobbling around and making lots of
noise. We're all worried about what
Mr Pinch is going to say when he sees
them!"

Zoe saw what the keeper meant. As the orangutans, hippos and elephants came into view, she realised they were all stumbling from side to side – and screeching, grunting or trumpeting with laughter. Quickly she ran over to Hetty, the smallest

hippo. "What's going on, Hetty?" she whispered.

Hetty's eyes were bright with excitement as she grunted back to Zoe.

"You're all copying *Jamie*?" said Zoe, looking around for the little giraffe.

"He's over there, Zoe!" cried Meep.

As the tallest animals in the zoo, the giraffes came right at the end of the parade.

There at the front was the mischievous baby giraffe, who was wobbling on his spindly legs more than ever! Jewel was walking gracefully beside him, but all the other big animals were watching the little calf's antics and copying him!

Zoe groaned. It did look very funny but the animals were about to walk past the strict zoo manager, and she knew he wasn't going to be impressed.

"What on earth is going on here?" snapped Mr Pinch, his face turning bright pink. "I said I wanted a nice, neat, tidy and well-behaved line. This is utter chaos!"

"Is everything all right, Mr Pinch?" asked Lucy, who had heard the commotion and come running over.

"No, everything is not all right!" cried

Mr Pinch. "These animals are going to turn my lovely parade into a shambles. How are we supposed to win the Best Zoo Award with terrible behaviour like this?" He pointed a shaking finger at the giggling baby giraffe. "And I know which animal is to blame. Ever since that naughty giraffe was born, the other animals have been out of control. Well, I won't have it. If he can't learn to behave, he won't be allowed in the parade at all!"

As Mr Pinch stomped off, Zoe sighed. She loved the gorgeous baby giraffe, but his tricks were starting to become a big problem! *How can I get him to behave?* she thought to herself. *There must be something I can do.*

Chapter Five
The Best Zoo

"It's today! It's today!" chattered Meep excitedly as he scampered along the footpath.

Zoe and Meep were on their way to see Jamie. It was Saturday morning, and the day of the judges' visit to the Rescue Zoo.

Zoe thought that she'd never seen the zoo look so lovely. The paths were swept

and the fences were freshly painted.
Bunches of colourful balloons were tied
to the trees, and extra-bright flowers had
been planted everywhere. The zoo was
already full of excited visitors, who were
queuing up on the paths to watch the
parade.

But Zoe was worried. She had tried
talking to the funny little giraffe about his
behaviour after the practice parade a few
days ago, but he hadn't seemed to listen.
He was having too much fun. This was
her last chance to convince him to behave
well.

When Jamie saw Zoe and Meep slip
inside his enclosure he trotted over
excitedly and nuzzled his soft head against
Zoe's hand.

"Hi, Jamie," said Zoe, stroking his

snout. "I wanted to talk to you about the parade later today. We were wondering—"

Meep burst out laughing as the cheeky giraffe stuck out his long, pointy, purple tongue. "Meep!" cried Zoe as the little lemur copied him and stuck out his own tiny pink tongue. "That's not very helpful, is it?"

"Sorry, Zoe," Meep chirped sheepishly.

Zoe turned back to the baby giraffe. "Anyway, Jamie – Meep and I wanted to talk to you about the parade. We think it would be really good if you behaved nicely, because Mr Pinch is going to—"

Jamie poked out his tongue again, and Meep giggled again. Zoe sighed. *This isn't going to work*, she thought. *Jamie isn't listening – and Meep's just getting distracted!*

Just then, Theo the giraffe keeper arrived at the enclosure. "Hi, Zoe!" he called. "The judges have just arrived. They want to see all the animals in their enclosures before we start the parade. There are three of them, and they all look quite strict, just like Mr Pinch."

Zoe took a deep breath. *This is going to be a disaster*, she thought. But to Zoe's relief, Jamie seemed to be behaving himself as he calmly trotted over to Theo and the other giraffes. "He's behaving himself for now, at least," Zoe muttered to herself. She really hoped it would continue.

"Here come the judges!" whispered Theo.

Zoe peered down the path and saw three people in smart suits, all holding

clipboards and pens. One of them, a
stern-looking lady with short grey hair
and green glasses, had a badge pinned
to her jacket that said "HEAD JUDGE".
A nervous-looking Mr Pinch was leading
them. Great-Uncle Horace and Lucy
were there too. Zoe hurried out of the
giraffe enclosure to join them.

"Here goes," Zoe whispered to Meep,
who was perched on her shoulder, waving
his tiny paws excitedly. "I hope Jamie
remembers to be good!"

The judges strolled down the path,
looking carefully at the animals as
they passed, and making notes on their
clipboards. Zoe saw the head judge pay
special attention to the enclosures, too.
"Very impressive," she heard her say as
she studied the polar bears' home, which

was a huge, twinkling igloo with a deep
blue pool for Bella and Snowy, the two
gorgeous polar bears, to splash around in.

Next, the head judge peered over
the fence at the penguins. Some of
the penguins were happily diving and
swooping in their pool, catching shiny
fish in their beaks. Other penguins sunned
themselves on the smooth rocks around
the edge of the enclosure. Zoe saw the
head judge smile and nod.

Zoe's heart leapt. This was going well!
The judges seemed to like the zoo – and
the animals were being as good as gold.

"Oh, the giraffes!" the head judge said,
peering down the path and spotting the
enclosure. "I've heard excellent things
about the Rescue Zoo giraffe enclosure.
I'd like to take a look at that next."

"Of course! Right this way," said Great-Uncle Horace, leading her to the enclosure.

Zoe's heart began to pound. *Please, please be good, Jamie*, she thought to herself.

The judges walked up to the fence and looked inside. "Goodness me. What a beautiful home," the head judge said approvingly. "And such elegant creatures. I hear you have a new baby giraffe here at the zoo?"

"Indeed we do!" said Great-Uncle Horace, pointing at Jamie. "Here he is."

Jamie trotted towards the fence curiously and lowered his neck so that his head was right next to the judge's. Zoe swallowed nervously, and thought she saw Mr Pinch doing the same. *Don't let us down, Jamie!* she thought.

But in one quick movement, the little
giraffe stuck out his long purple tongue –
and grabbed the lady's glasses from
her face!

"Jamie, no!" said Zoe quickly – but it was too late. The naughty calf popped the glasses on top of his head. The crowds of zoo visitors who were lining the path to watch the parade all burst out laughing.

But the judge didn't seem to find it very funny. "My glasses!" she cried, frowning at Jamie.

"Jamie, give those back right now," whispered Zoe, holding out her hand.

But the giggly giraffe was having way too much fun with the glasses to pay any attention to Zoe. He waved his head back and forth – making the visitors laugh even more! Then he shook his head so hard the glasses went flying up into the air and over the fence. Thankfully Zoe was able to catch them.

"Here you go," she said, handing the

The Giggly Giraffe

glasses back to
the head judge.
She watched
anxiously as
the head judge
put her glasses
back on and
wrote something
on her clipboard.
She seemed *very*
unimpressed. Had
Jamie just spoiled the
Rescue Zoo's chances of
winning the prize?

Mr Pinch's face turned very red. "Er,
time to start the parade!" he announced
quickly. "I think you'll like this very
much, madam," he added to the head
judge.

"Hmm," muttered the head judge, looking stern.

The zoo keepers began leading the animals out of their enclosures and into their line, under the watchful eye of Mr Pinch. As the parade began, Zoe crossed her fingers. Slowly and steadily, the line of animals marched past the judges, who all nodded and whispered to one another. Zoe wished she could overhear what they were saying! *If I could just get a peep at their clipboards, I might be able to read what they've written down*, she thought, edging a bit nearer to them and standing on her tiptoes.

"Well, I never!" the head judge exclaimed.

Zoe looked up – and gasped. The animals parading past the judges were sticking out their tongues! Zoe groaned as she turned to see Jamie pulling funny faces. The other animals were all copying him and pulling funny faces too. The monkeys blew raspberries and the hippos waggled their tongues from side to side.

As the judges stared, the parade of animals burst out laughing together. The neat, tidy and calm line suddenly became the noisiest pack of cackling, chuckling, braying and squawking animals Zoe had ever heard!

Without thinking, Zoe darted towards Jamie. She squeezed through the line of giggling animals until she was standing next to him. "Jamie," she whispered. "You've got to stop making all the animals laugh. Mr Pinch is going to be so cross – and the judges are going think this is the worst zoo they've ever seen!"

"I should have known *you* were behind this," snapped a cross voice.

Zoe turned round and saw Mr Pinch glaring at her, his hands on his hips. "You made them all overexcited, didn't you?"

"No!" cried Zoe. "It wasn't me!"

"Mr Pinch, I think we've seen enough," called the head judge. "We'll go to the zoo café to make our final decision. We won't be very long."

Mr Pinch stared helplessly after the judges as they walked away. "Well, there goes our chance of winning the award," he said miserably. "We've blown it!" He scowled at Zoe. "Did you know the prize money could have paid for us to make our animal enclosures even better? I was going to get a waterslide for the penguins and a new climbing frame for the monkeys. But it will all go to another zoo now!"

Chapter Six
Giraffe Ice Creams

As Mr Pinch stormed away, ordering the
keepers to take all the animals back to
their enclosures, Zoe's heart sank. She had
done her best to persuade the little giraffe
to be good but it hadn't worked. She
looked at Meep and sighed. "Oh, Meep,
I feel awful about not winning the prize
money. I didn't even know there *was* prize

money. It would have been lovely to be able to make our animal enclosures even better, wouldn't it?"

Meep nodded sadly.

Next to Zoe, Jamie had finally stopped giggling. Instead, he was looking as unhappy as Zoe felt.

His long neck drooped and his dark, shiny eyes were full of sadness. He nudged Zoe with his nose and let out a miserable bleat.

Zoe managed a smile. "That's OK, Jamie," she whispered. "It doesn't matter."

Jamie gave another sad bleat. Zoe listened carefully as the little giraffe explained why he'd been behaving so crazily. When he'd finished, she shook her head. "Oh, Jamie! You didn't need to mess around and be silly to make friends at the zoo," she said gently. "Everyone here would have loved you just as much, even if you didn't make them laugh."

"Well, *almost* as much," added Meep, from Zoe's shoulder.

"Meep, that's not very helpful," whispered Zoe.

"Sorry!" squeaked Meep.

"Look – I'll prove it to you," Zoe told the little giraffe. "Come with me."

She led Jamie along the path to a nearby enclosure. Inside, the brown bears were relaxing in the sunshine, and the two cubs, Billy and Buzz, were playing with a ball. When they saw Zoe their eyes lit up. "Hi, everyone!" called Zoe, waving. "Jamie and I thought we'd come by and say hello."

She whispered to Jamie, "Now, try saying hello to the bears – but remember, just be yourself. You don't need to act silly or make them laugh for them to like you."

Jamie nodded nervously. Then he took a deep breath and greeted the cubs. He stared in surprise as the bears gave him a warm, friendly grunt back, and the two cubs raised their paws and waved.

"You see?" said Zoe, grinning. "The bears like you just as much as before. Didn't I tell you? Let's try another enclosure now."

They walked on to the penguin enclosure and peered over the fence. A bit more bravely than last time, Jamie called hello to the colony – and beamed in delight as all the penguins waved their flippers and squawked back. They were obviously very pleased to see him.

"There," said Zoe, stroking Jamie gently on his neck. "Well done, Jamie. I knew you could do it. Now, there's one last place we need to go. Follow me."

Zoe led the way down the path. She smiled as she saw the little giraffe taking slow, careful, steady steps on his long, spindly legs, with no wobbling or stumbling at all.

Suddenly Meep squeaked, "I think I know where we're going. The zoo café!"

"That's right, Meep," replied Zoe.

Jamie gave a worried bleat, and Zoe nodded. "Yes, the judges *are* there. We're going to show them how well behaved you can be. I have an idea."

Quickly, she whispered in the little giraffe's ear.

When they turned the next corner, Zoe saw the three judges sitting at a table by the window of the zoo café, with their clipboards and pens in front of them. They looked like they were having a very serious discussion. "Come on," she said to Jamie.

She stepped inside the café and saw the look of surprise on the judges' faces as Jamie stepped in after her, lowering his head and neck so that he would fit through the door.

The other visitors in the café all cheered with delight.

"Hello," Zoe said to the judges. "We know you're busy, but we just wanted to come and make you a special Rescue Zoo treat."

Quickly, she slipped behind the counter

of the café, where the ice cream was
kept. She grabbed an ice-cream scoop
and three bowls, and put a big scoop
of banana ice cream in each one. Then
she smiled at the baby giraffe. "This is
the bit I need your help for, Jamie," she
whispered.

Zoe and the judges watched as Jamie
stretched his neck up. He reached towards
a high shelf, far above Zoe's head,
where packets of ingredients were piled.
Carefully, he stuck his long tongue out
and curled it around a bag of chocolate
buttons, picking it up off the shelf. Then,
lowering his neck, he dropped the bag
into Zoe's hands.

"Thanks, Jamie!" laughed Zoe.

She scattered chocolate buttons over the
ice creams, then put a long silver spoon

in each bowl and placed them on a tray.
Then she carried the tray over to the
judges' table.

"Giraffe ice creams," she explained
proudly, handing one to each judge.
"We hope you like them. We wanted to
say sorry for Jamie taking your glasses

before," she added to the head judge. "He's only a week old, and very playful, but he didn't mean any harm."

To her relief, the head judge beamed. "Giraffe ice creams – what a treat!" she exclaimed. "Thank you very much. This looks absolutely delicious. And you mustn't worry about the glasses. Actually, we all thought it was very funny."

"You did?" Zoe stared at her in surprise.

The judge ate a spoonful of ice cream and nodded. "Just as I thought – absolutely delicious! Now, we're almost ready to come and tell you all our decision, so why don't you show us the way back?"

101

When the judges had finished eating their ice creams, Zoe led them back along the path to where Mr Pinch, Lucy, Great-Uncle Horace and the zoo keepers were waiting.

Mr Pinch's mouth dropped open in shock as he saw them arriving with Jamie beside them. "What is that animal doing out of its enclosure?" he spluttered. "And walking with the judges? After all the trouble it's caused already—"

"Mr Pinch, I'm pleased to say that we've reached our decision," interrupted the head judge.

Everyone waited in silence. Zoe held her breath and crossed both sets of fingers tight.

"You should all be very proud of your zoo," the judge went on. "Not only is it beautiful, but your animals are quite remarkable. In fact, we have never seen such happy animals before. This little chap is a perfect example," she added, nodding at Jamie.

Zoe glanced at Mr Pinch, whose eyes looked like they were about to pop out of his head.

"And that is why we have decided that you are the winners of the Best Zoo Award!" the judge said with a smile. "Perhaps *you* should look after this, my dear." She pulled a shiny gold trophy from her bag and handed it to Zoe.

Everyone cheered and clapped.

Zoe couldn't believe it. "We've won!" she cried.

"I ... I just don't know what to say," stuttered Mr Pinch, who looked as if he

wasn't sure whether to laugh or cry. "Manager of the Best Zoo – *me*!"

"We mustn't forget the prize money," added the head judge, handing Mr Pinch a gold envelope. "Congratulations! We're sure you will do excellent things with it."

"This is just splendid," said Great-Uncle Horace, beaming. "I'm very proud of you all – every single person *and* animal at the Rescue Zoo. Now, we must think of a good way to celebrate. But what?"

Zoe knew! "Giraffe ice creams!" she cried. "Wait there – we'll go and get them!"

Zoe, Meep and Jamie raced down the path, back towards the zoo café. Meep used his nimble fingers to line up enough bowls for everyone, and Zoe added the scoops of banana ice cream, while

Jamie held the bag of chocolate buttons
between his teeth and scattered a few into
each bowl. Then Zoe found a big trolley
that was used whenever parties were held
at the zoo, and stacked the bowls on top.
With some help from Jamie, she pushed
the trolley back towards the waiting
crowd.

"Giraffe ice creams for everyone!" she
cried, handing them out.

As everyone ate their ice creams,
Zoe whispered to Meep, "can you start
spreading the word to the animals that
we've won the prize? Everyone's going to
be so happy!"

Meep nodded and scampered off. Soon
Zoe heard an excited chatter start passing
through the zoo enclosures, as the good
news spread. She felt a warm tingling in

her tummy. It seemed like everyone in the
whole zoo was celebrating together!

When the ice creams were finished, and
the judges had left the zoo, it was time for
Jamie to go back to his enclosure.

"Wait until your mum hears what the judges said about you," Zoe whispered to him, giving him a cuddle. "She's going to be so proud of you!"

As an excited Jamie stepped into his enclosure, his legs wobbled and he almost tripped over his own feet!

The other giraffes began giggling – and so did the elephants and the monkeys, from their own enclosures close by. Jamie shot Zoe a very worried glance.

Zoe grinned. "I know that was an accident, Jamie!" she said. "And you don't need to look so worried. It's good to make people laugh – sometimes!"

If you enjoyed Jamie's story,
look out for:

Chapter One

A Snowy Surprise

Zoe Parker wrapped her woolly scarf snugly round her neck and brushed a flurry of snowflakes from the front of her coat.

"Brrr! It feels so wintry today!" she said, shivering.

"Well, it *is* the start of December," replied her mum, Lucy, smiling and rubbing her hands together to stay warm.

"It's my favourite time of year," added Zoe's Great-Uncle Horace. "And today is the perfect day for a walk with my two favourite people! The Rescue Zoo always looks rather magical with a dusting of snow and a few Christmas lights. Don't you think, Zoe?"

Zoe grinned at him. "Definitely!" she said, reaching out to hold hands with him through her mittens. "I love this time of year too. I'm so glad you're back for Christmas and New Year, Great-Uncle Horace."

"So am I, Zoe!" Great-Uncle Horace replied, beaming. "I do love going on adventures around the world, but there really is no place quite like home. Especially at Christmas time!"

Just as he said this, there was a very noisy trumpeting sound behind them. Zoe spun round to see Bertie, the cheeky young elephant, inside his enclosure.

Great-Uncle Horace chuckled. "And it sounds like Bertie is pleased too," he added, winking at Zoe.

Zoe giggled at the funny little elephant. Going out for an early Sunday morning stroll was always lots of fun when you had a very special home, like Zoe did. She and her family weren't just visiting the Rescue Zoo – they actually lived there!

Great-Uncle Horace was a famous explorer and animal expert. He had met so many lost, injured and endangered animals on his travels that he had decided to set up the Rescue Zoo. Now it was a safe home for hundreds of animals that had needed help, just like Bertie.

Zoe's mum, Lucy, was Great-Uncle Horace's niece and the Rescue Zoo vet. Because she needed to be close to the animals at all times in case of an emergency, she and Zoe lived in a little cottage just at the edge of the zoo. This meant that Zoe was only ever a few minutes away from all her favourite animals. Zoe's bedroom window even looked out on the enclosures, so she woke up every morning to the sound of the animals squawking, roaring and grunting!

Just like her mum and great-uncle, Zoe loved animals, and so she completely adored her amazing home. This morning it looked even more beautiful than usual.

It was a chilly day but the sky was very bright and blue. There was a light powdering of white snow on the branches of the trees and the red-brick path. Some of the zookeepers had hung garlands of holly, ivy and mistletoe along the fences, so that the zoo would look extra-specially festive when the gates opened to the visitors later that morning.

As they walked on, there was a tiny squeak from inside Zoe's coat. A grey, furry little head with fuzzy ears and big eyes popped out above her collar. "Is it time for lunch yet, Zoe? We've been walking for ages and ages!"

Zoe nuzzled the soft, fluffy head with her cheek. "No we haven't, Meep! And we've only just eaten breakfast!" she whispered with a smile, being careful not to let her mum and Great-Uncle Horace overhear. "And *you* haven't been doing any walking. You've been cuddled up inside my coat since we left home!"

"That's because I want to stay nice and warm!" squeaked Meep. "I don't like walking on the snow. It makes my paws cold."

On her sixth birthday, Zoe had discovered something magical. She had found out that animals can understand people, and can talk to them. Most people don't understand animals, but Zoe had found out that she *could*! It was Zoe's most special secret. She'd never told another person – not even her mum!

Her amazing gift had made growing up in a zoo even more fun. Whenever no one else was around, Zoe loved chatting

with the animals, from the tiniest tree frog
to the biggest hippopotamus. And of all
the animals at the Rescue Zoo, Meep was
her favourite. He was a tiny grey mouse
lemur, with huge golden eyes, an adorable
little nose and a long, curling tail. Unlike
all the other animals at the zoo, Meep
lived in the cottage with Zoe and her
mum. He and Zoe went everywhere
together.

Zoe dug deep in her coat pocket and
pulled out a handful of seeds. "I thought
you might get hungry," she whispered
to Meep, "so I brought along a snack for
you, just in case." She giggled as Meep
stuffed the nuts and seeds straight into his
mouth, making his cheeks puff up like a
hamster.

"Zoe, why don't we head out of the zoo

today?" suggested Great-Uncle Horace. "There's always lots of wonderful wildlife in the woods."

"OK!" replied Zoe with a smile. She followed the path round to the right, past the koalas and the flying foxes, towards a side gate that led out of the zoo and into some woodland. Great-Uncle Horace looked after the woods too, but they weren't part of the zoo grounds. And, unlike the zoo, they were left to grow wild. Zoe found the woodland mysterious and exciting!

She stepped carefully through the snowy bushes, keeping an eye out for any movement. Zoe knew that the field mice and hedgehogs would be hibernating at this time of year, but there would still be wild rabbits and hares running about, as well as pheasants.

Great-Uncle Horace glanced up and whistled to a large vivid-blue bird with huge feathery wings, flying along above them. At his whistle, she swooped down through the trees and perched on his shoulder. This was Kiki, Great-Uncle Horace's hyacinth macaw. She went with him on all his travels.

Zoe's Rescue Zoo

Look out for MORE
amazing animal adventures
at the Rescue Zoo!

The Secret Rescuers

If you enjoyed this book,
we think you'll love The Secret Rescuers!

The Rescue Princesses

Have you read the brilliant Rescue Princesses books? And look out for NEW Rescue Princesses, coming soon.